Shadow Boy

David Beals

To order additional copies of this book, contact:
Xlibris
1-888-795-4274
www.Xlibris.com
Orders@Xlibris.com

I would like to dedicate this to my mom and dad,...
'To JoAnn and Bud For All the Love'

Many millions of years ago there was a very young universe Inhabited by a family of nine planets, one star, and many little moons. They were all greatly excited as Matra, the third planet in that universe was with life.

Matra's brother and sister planets were all very proud. She was looked upon with awe and respect by all of the heavenly bodies. She was the fertile garden blessed with this growing new spirit and the happy little planet twirled on her axis like a ballerina within the night.

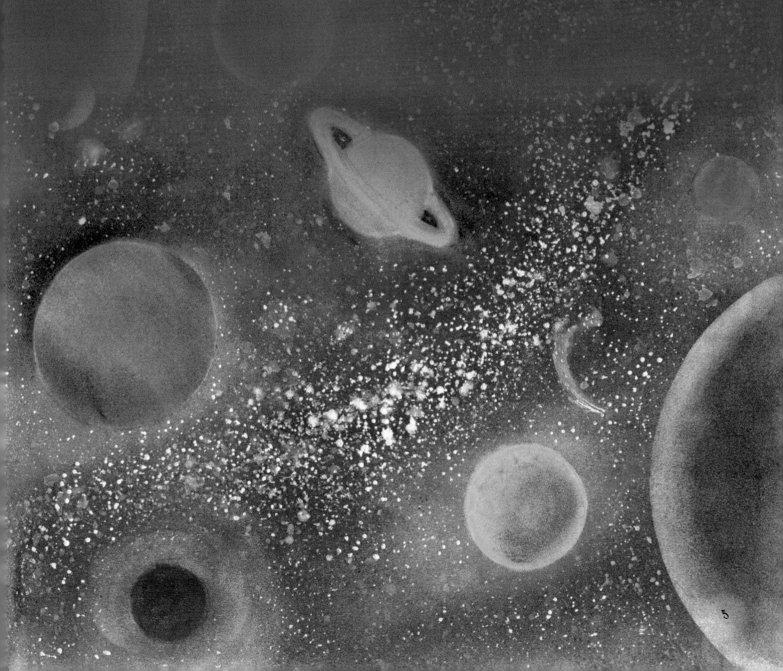

In time there evolved from that first life on Matra a walking, thinking, caring creature and they called him Shadow Boy. How he was loved by all of the heavens! He was loved almost as much as Matra , for he was filled with respect and reverence for Matra, whom he knew as his mother and indeed, for all of the creation.

All was well within the universe for many thousands of years, especially on Matra. Shadow Boy grew and was happy and content with his life on the little planet. One day however without any warning he became very ill. So ill in fact, it was thought that he might soon perish. The heavens were mystified and Matra wept and all who loved him awaited the end.

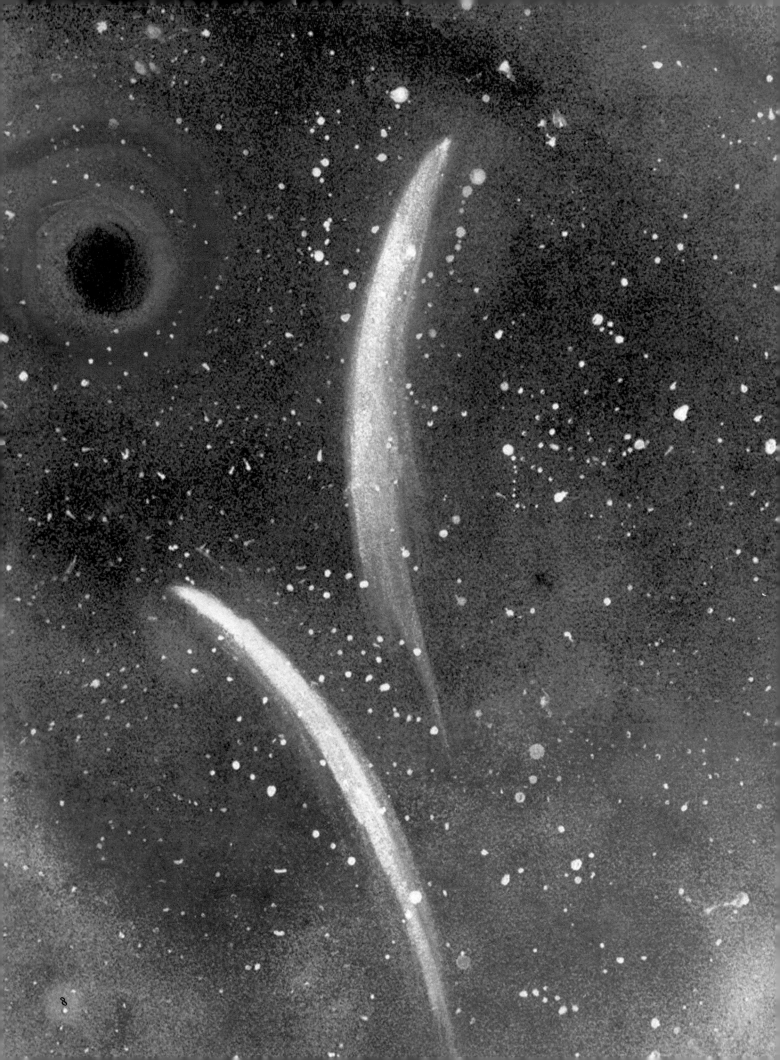

8

As Shadow Boy took what he thought might be his last breath a trio of long tailed stars streaked past. The dying creature made an unselfish and desperate wish upon them: he wished for another like himself who would continue to enjoy the immense beauty of the heavens and the love of his mother. Then he closed his tearful eyes and awaited the end. As he listened to the wind that blew over the plains and to the spinning of the orb that was his home, he waited and waited and waited and then heard... then heard? Why it... it was the light, cadenced breathing of another. It was the Other!!

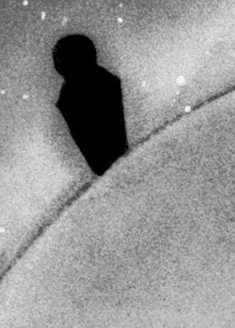

He could not believe it! What joy this moment brought to him and to Matra and to all in the heavens. Soon Shadow Boy began to heal and grew healthy again. The heavens rejoiced, and understood that with the Other, Shadow Boy was alone no more, nor was he lonely. Shadow Boy's wish had come to pass.

The Other was much like Shadow Boy In many ways. Side by side and hardly ever one without the other, they explored the vast plains of Matra for a thousand years. How they loved her and the endless reaches of creation they witnessed from upon her. There was always discovery in their eyes and wonder in their beings; about the heavens above, their souls within and about Matra who nurtured them as only a mother can do!

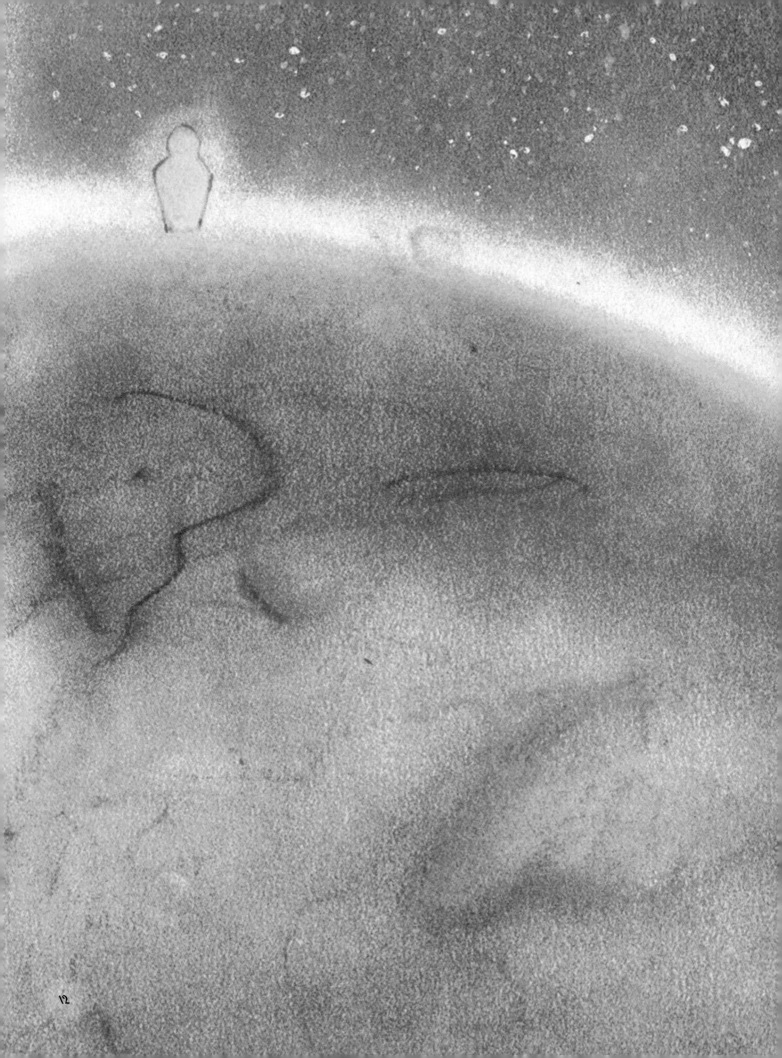

One day however, the Other came to Shadow Boy with a very odd thought and spoke.

"Brother! Why don't we do something that we've not done before? Something new, and exciting! Why don't you go one way across those plains and I will go the other way and we'll meet soon on the other side of Matra?" He pleaded with a smile. Shadow Boy's eyes filled with tears.

"Oh no!" he cried. "There is no reason for that. That will never do." He would have nothing to do with that idea. But the Other thought it was a great plan and finally had his way.

For the first time in over a thousand years the two brothers parted ways. Unknown to all who witnessed this day, it was to be another thousand years before the two would meet again.

It was a fine night, that special night many, many years later as Matra plied her way through the oceans of the universe. Above, the heavens shimmered and shined as they rejoiced in seeing the happy and festive reunion when the two met again.

"Oh brother I've missed you so," they exclaimed to one another, "and we will part no more!" But something had changed, for Shadow Boy and the Other both had large families following along behind them. There were so very many of each of them they had to come up with a plan as to how they all could live on Matra as one. It was decided that Shadow Boy and his clan would live on one half of Matra, and the Other and his would live on the other half. This idea worked out fine for the longest time, until one day...

"We have a problem, old friend." spoke the Other. "We've grown so much in number that we are running out of room on our side of Matra!"

"This is a problem", agreed Shadow Boy, "for we are crowded too." Shadow Boy sounded fearful.

"This is not good !" And it was not for the leaders of the two clans could not agree on how to solve the problem. They began to get angry. The anger grew and grew as the open and free plains began to fill with all of the creatures. One day the two clans began to fight, and to chase each other around Matra.

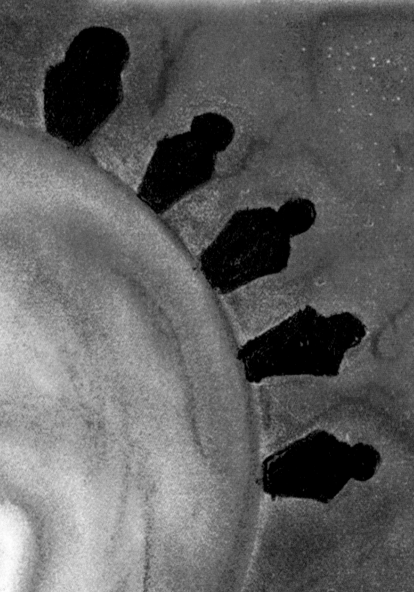

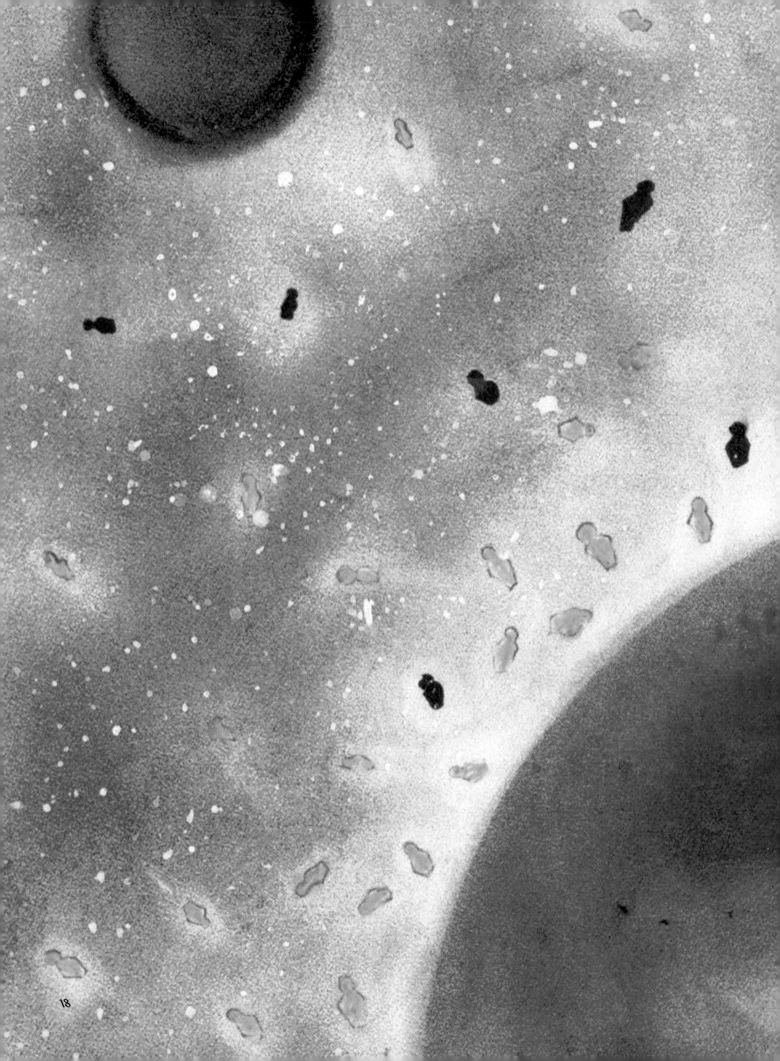

A great hush fell over the heavens as they watched Shadow Boys and Others go round and round, faster and faster and faster still with no regard for any but themselves. In time Matra began to crumble beneath their feet. By the two's and by the dozens the creatures fell off the planet and out into space. Matra grew smaller and smaller until all that was left was one solitary creature. It was Shadow Boy upon the tiny core of what was once Matra!

"Look what we've done to you!" he cried. "And it can't be undone!" Shadow Boy was very sad and all alone. Amid tears and farewell Matra began to move away from her familiar path and soon drifted beyond her family and out towards the far reaches of the heavens. The universe wept.

22

Epilogue

This is not the end of our story however, but simply the beginning. About a million years or so after the Shadow Boys and the Others had broken the hearts of so many by destroying Matra, another family of nine planets, one star, and many little moons were very excited. Life had come to one of theirs.

It seems that one of the crumbled pieces of Matra has passed through this universe and had fallen on the planet known as Earth. That fragment had survived and grown and Matra, once the garden had become the seed.

At this very moment on Matra, and on what is Earth's moon, the solitary figure of Shadow Boy quietly and caringly watches his garden grow. As he does he recalls Matra's beauty,

but most of all, her kindness and her love.

And Shadow Boy, who now has all of us to keep him company, understands full and well that it is because of that love that the Earth now twirls on her axis like a ballerina within the night

THE END